MW00951913

CHARLIE, TEDDY & ROAR
IreLaNd

by Melissa Brandon
Illustrated by Julie Sneeden

Dedication

To CJB and TJB

I love you both - to UY Scuti and back.

In a lemon colored house,
   that's just right next door
Live my good friends,
   Teddy, Charlie and Roar

Teddy is three
    and really quite clever
Charlie is five
    and brighter than ever

But Roar, well he's different, one just might say
He's Teddy's best friend with an adventurous way

Every afternoon when the kids
come home to play
Roar takes them out
for a magical day

The latest adventure they told me about
Took them over the Atlantic to go check it out

They brought home stories of
a land vibrant and green
With shamrocks and limericks
and rainbows that gleam

"It's a country called Ireland,"
Charlie implored
"With a park called St. Stephen's
that we got to explore."

"We even saw leprachauns,"
Roar said with a shimmer
"And a big pot of gold
that really did glimmer."

"But wait!" the kids said
"That's not the best part."
"What is it?" I wondered
"Food? Music? Art?"

"No," laughed Charlie
   "Not quite," chuckled Teddy
"We don't think you've seen it -
   are you sure that you're ready?"

"Our favorite part
   was giant and green!"
"It was the biggest bus
   that we've ever seen."

"A double decker!" I chortled, chuckled and grinned
"What a wonderful trip, I've never been!"

"It's all thanks to Roar,"
Teddy said with a smile
"With our imaginations,
we can go miles."

"But wait," Roar whispered,
"that's just the start."
"I'm full of adventure.
It's what's in my heart."

.... Where to next?

CPSIA information can be obtained
at www.ICGtesting.com
Printed in the USA
LVHW070844111220
672560LV00043B/224